Bubble & Squeak

by
Louise Bonnett-Rampersaud

illustrated by
Susan Banta

Marshall Cavendish Children

Marshall Cavendish Corporation, 99 White Plains Road, Tarrytown, NY 10591
www.marshallcavendish.us

Library of Congress Cataloging-in-Publication Data
Bonnett-Rampersaud, Louise.
Bubble and Squeak / by Louise Bonnett-Rampersaud ; illustrated by Susan Banta. — 1st ed.
p. cm.
Summary: Bubble helps her mother practice bedtime rituals, such as checking for monsters and reading a favorite book,
that Bubble proclaims she has outgrown,
but that her baby sister, Squeak, will need when she gets a little older.
ISBN-13: 978-0-7614-5310-9
ISBN-10: 0-7614-5310-5
[1. Bedtime—Fiction. 2. Mothers and daughters—Fiction. 3. Sisters—Fiction.] I. Banta, Susan, ill. II. Title.
PZ7.B642534Bub 2006
[E]—dc22
2005027933

The text of this book is set in Bulmer MT.
The illustrations are rendered in acrylics.
Book design by Anahid Hamparian

Printed in China

First edition
1 3 5 6 4 2

mc Marshall Cavendish
Children

Thanks for everything this year. You know who you are.
—L. B.-R.

For my mother
—S. F. B.

Bubble climbed into bed.

Her still-sort-of-new baby sister, Squeak, was already asleep in her own room.

"Mom," Bubble said. "I was just wondering. When Squeak gets a little older and you're putting *her* to bed, what will you do if she's afraid of monsters in her room?"

"Monsters?" her mother asked.

"Well, *I'm* a big sister now, so *I'm* not afraid of them," Bubble said. "But . . . *she* might be."

"Hmmm," said her mother. "What do *you* think I should do about it?"

"I think you should check her closet," said Bubble.

"Like this?" her mother asked, as she opened Bubble's closet and looked up and down and all around.

Bubble nodded.

"And maybe you should check under her bed, too," she said. "Just to be *really* sure."

"Like this?" her mother asked, as she lifted up Bubble's bed skirt and checked for monsters.

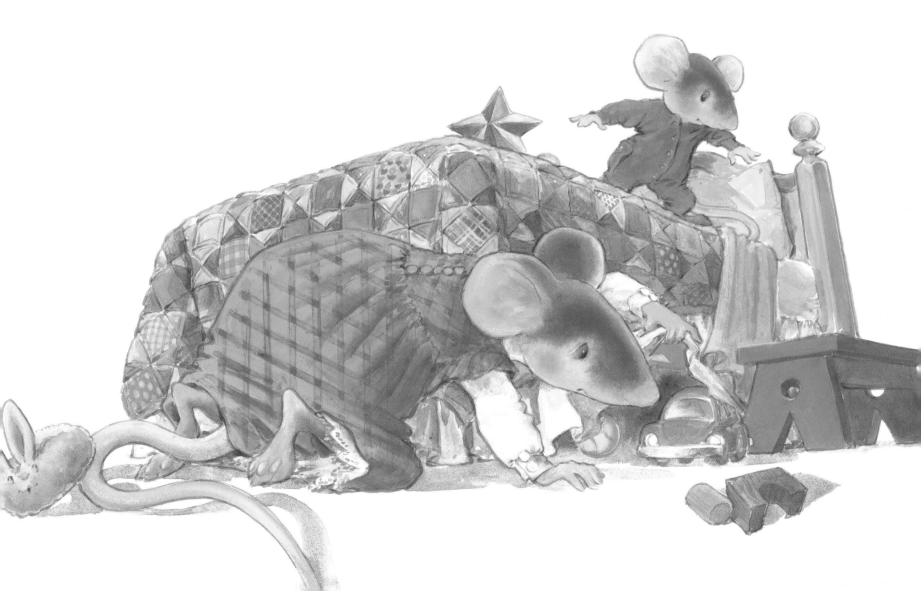

"Yes," Bubble said, with a smile on her face.

"*Just* like that."

"It's a good thing we figured that out," Bubble's mom said, as she bent down to give her a kiss good night. "Squeak will be very glad. Good night then, Bubble," and she tiptoed across the room.

But before her mom reached the door, Bubble said, "And, Mom, what if Squeak is also afraid of the dark when she's trying to fall asleep? What will you do then?"

"Since you're the big sister, you might know what would help her."

"This," Bubble said, holding
up her favorite bedtime book.
"I bet if you read her this story,
it would help. You can practice
reading to me if you'd like."

"Like this?" her mom asked,
as she climbed on the bed
and read to Bubble in a
soothing voice.

"Yes," Bubble said, with a smile on her face. "*Just* like that."

"And you know what else, Mom? I bet it would also help Squeak if you turned on her night-light before you left the room."

"Now that *is* a good idea," Bubble's mom said. "Mind if I turn on yours? Just to practice, of course."

"Sure," said Bubble, as she watched her mom turn on her night-light.

"Good night, now, Bubble," said her mom. "Sleep tight," and she quietly left the room.

But a few minutes later, so did Bubble.
She tiptoed along the hallway.

She scurried down the stairs.

And she crept into the kitchen.

"Bubble," her mom said, turning away from the sink. "What are you doing out of bed? I thought you'd be fast asleep by now."

"Well, I would have been," said Bubble. "It's just that I got to thinking . . . what if Squeak wakes up one night and she's thirsty, what will she be able to have to drink?"

"To drink?" her mom asked, as she walked over to the refrigerator. "How about some milk?"

"No, I don't . . . I mean, Squeak probably won't like milk," Bubble said quickly.

"Then what about juice?" her mom asked.

"Oh, no, definitely not juice," Bubble said.

"How about water then?" her mom asked.

"No, but you know what would be absolutely perfect for Squeak? You know that creamy, triple chocolaty hot chocolate you make?"

"Oh, you mean the kind with the little marshmallows sprinkled on top that look like a snowman?" said Bubble's mom.

Bubble's eyes lit up. "Yes!" she shouted with excitement. "That kind. That's the kind that will help Squeak."

"Well, since you're already up, would you like to try a cup yourself?" Bubble's mom asked. "Just to make sure it will meet with Squeak's approval, of course."

"Yes, please," Bubble said. And they took their hot chocolate and nestled down cozy snug in the chair that was the perfect size for a mom and a still-sort-of-new big sister.

"Do you think that will help her?" Bubble's mom asked, as they sipped their drinks and sang lullabies.

But Bubble was too cozy and snug to answer.
She was starting to fall asleep.

"I think that will definitely help." Bubble's mom chuckled
to herself when Bubble's eyes finally closed. "That will
definitely help Squeak."

And she bent down and gave Bubble a kiss good night.